Big Two-Hearted River

THE CENTENNIAL EDITION

Ernest Hemingway

Big Two-Hearted River

FOREWORD BY
John N. Maclean

ILLUSTRATIONS BY
Chris Wormell

MARINER CLASSICS
New York   Boston

This is a work of fiction. Names, characters, places, and incidents are products of the author's imagination or are used fictitiously and are not to be construed as real. Any resemblance to actual events, locales, organizations, or persons, living or dead, is entirely coincidental.

FIRST MARINER CLASSICS EDITION PUBLISHED 2023

DESIGNED BY *Lucy Albanese*

ILLUSTRATIONS BY *Chris Wormell*

Library of Congress Cataloging-in-Publication Data has been applied for.

ISBN 978-0-06-329749-4

24 25 26 27 28 LBC 9 8 7 6 5

CONTENTS

LIST OF ENGRAVINGS

The Boy, the War, and the Big Two-Hearted River

When I was a youngster struggling to reconcile a life split between a great community of learning in the Midwest and a log cabin in Montana, my father gave me Ernest Hemingway's "Big Two-Hearted River" to read. The story came as a revelation. My parents hailed from Montana, where we spent our summers, and they both worked at the University of Chicago, my father as a professor of English and my mother as an administrator for the university's medical center. Hemingway's tale evoked the core activity of our life in Montana: trout fishing.

It put you hip-deep in a river with Nick Adams, Hemingway's literary twin, a cold current throbbing against your thighs. You tasted the humidity in the air above the river, a second stream thick with insect life and a sweet musk smell from the enclosing brush. The story virtually put the rod in your hand to fight a big fish. Best of all for me, it bridged the gap between my two worlds and brought trout fishing to life through literature.

Hemingway, too, was young and living in contrasting worlds when he wrote "Big Two-Hearted River." He was just twenty-five when he sat down in a Paris café to work on a story based on a fishing trip a few years earlier to Michigan's Upper Peninsula—the UP—with two friends, Jack Pentecost and Al Walker. It was a heady time for the young, unproven writer, who had joined writers and artists of what came to be called the Lost Generation, along with the likes of F. Scott Fitzgerald,

Pablo Picasso, and Man Ray, as well as older artists like Ezra Pound and Gertrude Stein, who became his surrogate parents. His personal life, too, was packed with challenge and adventure. He had been wounded only a few years earlier as a Red Cross volunteer in Italy during the Great War, recuperated and returned home, gone fishing in the UP, married and moved to Paris with his new wife, Hadley Richardson, followed quickly by the birth of a son, Jack (or "Bumby"), and discovered a passion for bullfighting.

Hemingway wrote in cafés for the quiet. The fishing story he started with three handwritten pages—in a large, almost flowery script on typewriter stock—grew in halting stages, interrupted by other work and a trip to Spain for the bullfighting. As the drafts progressed, the two buddies disappeared and instead Nick Adams set off on a solo pilgrimage to ease a troubled mind with a fly rod.

The exact timing for when he wrote each part is hard to pin down—Hemingway couldn't recall it himself, and the drafts aren't dated—but from accounts by him and others, it appears he completed part 1 and was well into part 2 by late spring of 1924 before he headed to Pamplona for the running of the bulls. "The story was interrupted you know just when I was going good," he complained in a letter that fall.

When he got back to it in late summer or early fall, he'd lost the flow. In the new draft, Hemingway veered from the solo fishing trip in the UP into a long, rambling discourse on writing, writers, bull-fighting in Pamplona—and vaulting personal ambition: "He wanted to become a great writer," he wrote. "He was pretty sure he would be." By the fall of 1924, Hemingway had completed a manuscript, titled it "Big Two-Hearted River," and sent it off to a publisher for inclusion in his first real book,

In Our Time. He showed the manuscript to Stein, who said of the discourse on writing, "Hemingway, remarks are not literature." Jolted back to his old self, he reread the section at issue and called it "crap" and worse in letters to her and others. "I got a hell of a shock when I realized how bad it was," he wrote one correspondent. He ditched the almost ten-page section and had a new ending in the hands of his publisher before the presses rolled. It was a lucky catch: critics would not have been kind. The redone story first appeared in May 1925 in *This Quarter*, a Paris literary journal, and then in October as the anchor story for *In Our Time.* Despite complaints that "nothing happens" in the narrative, perceptive readers such as Edmund Wilson and F. Scott Fitzgerald hailed it as a masterpiece, albeit a short one.

"Because Big Two-Hearted River Is Poetry"

A century on, "Big Two-Hearted River" has helped shape language and literature in America and around the world, and its magnetic pull continues to draw readers, writers, and critics. It's the best early example of Hemingway's now-familiar writing style: short sentences, punchy nouns and verbs, few adjectives or adverbs, and a seductive cadence. Easy to imitate, difficult to match. The subject matter of the story has inspired generations of writers to believe that fly fishing can be literature, with mixed results. More than any of his stories, it depends on his "iceberg theory" of literature, the notion that leaving essential parts of a story unsaid adds to its power. Taken in context with his other work, it marks Hemingway's passage from boyish writer to accomplished author: nothing big came before it, novels and stories poured out after it.

After my dad gave me the story to read in the 1950s, we sat down together to analyze it. We were both deeply pleased that fishing and literature could be successfully combined, and in future decades we would strive to do the same thing as writers. But we stumbled over the meanings of the dark metaphors that begin and end the story. "Big Two-Hearted River" is not simply a luminous fishing tale; it's also an unsolved mystery. Like the title, the story has two sides, an outdoor adventure and the never-explained metaphors that accompany it, which have kept critics arguing ever since. As the narrative opens, Nick Adams steps off a train and discovers to his surprise that the old logging town of Seney has been burned over. Just what the scorched earth stands for is never stated, but it's not utter destruction. "It could not all be burned," Nick reflects as he hikes beyond the fire's black footprint into a meadow carpeted with sweet ferns and marked by hillocks with still-standing pines.

The great fires of the late nineteenth and early twentieth centuries burned across the north woods, supercharged by the wasteful logging practices of the day. Huge swaths of white pine were clear-cut and towns built on foundations of sawdust, perfect beds for the flames that followed, which indeed gutted several towns. Stumps from the logging remain visible to this day, poking up among the ferns. Several smaller fires burned around Seney just before Hemingway's 1919 trip, and he almost certainly walked through their black footprints.

In the story, as Nick shoulders his pack and sets off, he struggles with unnamed but troubling thoughts, hiking longer than necessary to deaden his mind and make sleep come more easily. He becomes absorbed in details of the moment as he makes camp, catches and loses fish, and explores his surroundings. As he watches trout rise, his spirit rises with them. He's repeatedly described as being happy, as though that, too, were a surprise. Then, after a day of fishing that includes a battle with the biggest trout he's ever seen, Nick faces a cedar swamp with deep swirling currents, a dark place similar to the burned landscape where the story began. "The fishing would be tragic," he tells himself, and repeats the thought: "In the swamp fishing was a tragic adventure." Nick has been on a journey of the spirit, however, and if the swamp holds unnamed terrors, they can be overcome. The story ends on another optimistic note: "There were plenty of days coming when he could fish the swamp."

When my father and I tried to make sense of the metaphors, we turned to other Nick Adams stories for clues. Hemingway wrote three stories about Nick having love affairs that end badly, all based on real events around the time of the 1919 fishing trip to the UP. "A Very Short Story" deals, in barely over a page, with a romance between a Nick-like character, who is never named, and an only slightly fictionalized Agnes von Kurowsky, a Red Cross nurse. She and Hemingway got together when she nursed him after he was wounded by shrapnel in his first days in Italy, delivering chocolate and other comforts by bicycle to soldiers at the front. After Hemingway returned home, Kurowsky wrote him a Dear Ernest letter to inform him she'd become engaged to an Italian nobleman. She was dumped, in turn, when the nobleman's family decided she was too common for their son. The story roughly follows these events and ends on a caustic note.

The other stories, "The End of Something" and "The Three-Day Blow," describe a romance with a

Michigan girl called Marge and Marjorie that re-
verses the roles: this time Nick is named, he does
the dumping, and the stories get longer. Hemingway met the real-life Marjorie, a teenaged redhead
with freckles, when she had a summer job as a
waitress at a restaurant on Walloon Lake, where
his family had a cabin. The handsome young war
hero and the pretty local girl both loved fishing and
good times, and they hit it off. In explaining to the
fictional Marjorie in "The End of Something" why
he's breaking up with her, Nick hints at an inner
darkness: "I feel as though everything was gone to
hell inside me." Sounds like a clue. The third story,
"The Three-Day Blow," is a conversation loosened
by drink between Nick and a buddy named Bill, at a
cottage in Michigan, about Nick's decision to break
up with Marjorie. The use of her first name made
Marjorie Bump a target of gossip in small-town
Michigan (her actual last name didn't help her

cause) and she eventually moved away. Although she and Hemingway were occasionally in touch in later years, the portrayal always bothered her and she burned their correspondence. But she also exchanged 250 letters about Hemingway with a determined researcher, and those survive.

My dad and I noted the breakups, but surely Nick had been trying to recover from more than a couple of youthful romances. Nonetheless, we virtually adopted the story into our family, we memorized lines from it, and both our writing styles owe Hemingway a debt. When my father published his first book, *A River Runs through It*, at the age of seventy-three, he was called a "garrulous Hemingway." I went on to work as a newspaperman, as Hemingway did, and as a cub reporter in Chicago with short vacations, I drove to the UP and fished the Big Two-Hearted River, an easier reach than Montana. True, the actual Hemingway trip was on the Fox River or a branch or two, but I chose the Big Two-Hearted for the same reason Hemingway made it the title of his story, for the poetry.

My career took me away from the Midwest, and I did not read Hemingway again for many decades. I returned to him when I wrote *Home Waters: A Chronicle of Family and a River*, which describes his influence on my father and me, only to find that we had missed the big shift in interpretation of "Big Two-Hearted River." I was invited to give a talk on *Home Waters* to The Community Library in Ketchum, Idaho, which acts as custodian of the historic Ernest and Mary Hemingway House, on the edge of town. In preparation, I reread "Big Two-Hearted River," which is mentioned in the book, and checked the modern commentary. It quickly became apparent that my dad and I had missed the likely solution to the metaphors. *The Nick Adams Stories*, published in 1972, for the first time placed the stories in chronological order for Nick. Several war stories written after "Big Two-Hearted River" now preceded it and offered an explanation for his troubled state of mind. One in particular, "A Way You'll Never Be," relates how Nick returned to the Italian front after being wounded and suffered a vividly described post-traumatic stress event. On top of that, in *A Moveable Feast* and in letters and an essay, Hemingway said the story was about a boy coming home troubled from the war.

His best explanation is in "The Art of the Short Story," a preface for a book of his stories commissioned by Charles Scribner, his publisher, who ultimately dropped the project. "Big Two-Hearted River," he said, "is about a boy coming home beat to the wide from a war. Beat to the wide was an earlier and possibly more severe form of beat, since those who had it were unable to comment on this condition and could not suffer that it be mentioned in their presence. So the war, all mention of the war, anything about the war, is omitted. The river was the Fox River, by Seney, Michigan, not the Big Two-Hearted. The change of name was made purposely, not from ignorance or carelessness but because Big Two-Hearted River is poetry."

The Nick Adams Stories, however, also contains the deleted section titled "On Writing," which prompted a heated, occasionally nasty debate among critics. Hemingway's latter-day efforts to make it a war story were just lies piled on other lies to buff his macho image, it was said. The story wasn't about the war at all; it was about Nick's raging desire to become a great writer. With that section deleted, the story came down to "No war, just the fishing," one critic remarked. The burned landscape and the desolate swamp in that case could stand for a writer's creative unconscious, forbidding but desirable.

For me, reconnecting with the story felt like discovering new depths in an old friend. In response, I set off on a cross-country journey to dig deeper and try to answer lingering questions such as: Was there hard evidence to be uncovered about what was troubling Nick, beyond Hemingway's claim that it was the war? Did Hemingway invent a fire-ravaged Seney? Where exactly did he and his friends fish? My travels led from the John F. Kennedy Presidential Library and Museum, in Boston, which has a vast Hemingway Collection, to Seney and the Fox River, in the UP, and finally to the Ernest and Mary Hemingway House, in Ketchum, where I was a guest for a week as writer in residence. At each stop I learned new things or answered a lingering question.

"The Old Feeling"

At the JFK Library's Ernest Hemingway Collection, I examined photocopies of the typed and handwritten drafts of "Big Two-Hearted River." In a very early version, there's a description of a flame-gutted hotel in Seney that strongly suggests the war was indeed on Hemingway's mind as he wrote the story. In this draft, one of his buddies, Al, sets off to investigate the damaged hotel, which is more like a World War I battlefield than a midwestern hostel. Called the Mansion House hotel in the story, the large wooden White House hotel in Seney actually burned down twice, once just before the Hemingway fishing trip. "Al went over and looked into the filled pit where the hotel had been. There was twisted iron work, melted too hard to rust. Thrown together were four gun barrels, pitted and twisted by the heat [and] in one the cartridges had melted in the magazine and formed a bulge of lead and copper." At last, the link to the war confirmed by the story itself, albeit a version that never made the final cut: the burned landscape and the dreary swamp, then, represent Nick's nightmarish memories of the war, and the all-engaging act of fishing helped put them to rest.

The drafts are remarkable, too, for the fluidity of the writing. The story grows longer and different versions are tried, but a near-final draft goes on for dozens of handwritten pages with hardly a later change. The story's power comes not just from mysterious metaphors but from inspired prose. Hemingway loved fishing from the time he was old enough to use a rod. In Paris, he was an ocean and more away from his home waters in Michigan. The separation intensified the writing. While he worked on the story, he kept a map of northern Michigan posted in his apartment, with blue marks for significant locations. In succeeding drafts, he stripped the story down to one disturbed person moving through a dreamlike, almost hallucinatory landscape of distorted reality. Brown grasshoppers evolve to black in the fire's footprint, a physical impossibility in the time between flames and green-up. Swamps are not known for being deep and full of swift currents; they are still and often shallow—the many swamps I saw around Seney certainly are. Words repeat, the rhythm pulses, and the prose becomes an incantation. In the following example, the words *sun, hot, trout, stream, shadow,* and *trees* appear again and again in short sentences, capped at the end by one long sentence that repeats nearly all those words, with hypnotic effect.

It was getting hot, the sun hot on the back of his neck.

Nick had one good trout. He did not care

about getting many trout. Now the stream was shallow and wide. There were trees along both banks. The trees of the left bank made short shadows on the current in the forenoon sun. Nick knew there were trout in each shadow. In the afternoon, after the sun had crossed toward the hills, the trout would be in the cool shadows on the other side of the stream.

Hemingway slightly varies this technique in one very long sentence, by his standards: an academic study found that the average length of a sentence in part 1 is twelve words, the average paragraph 105 words (minus three brief declarations by Nick that would skew the latter count). That's short by any standard. In the next example, the action could not be simpler: a large trout leaves shelter, breaks water, and returns to its place. It could be described in a few words, though the author adds a kingfisher to give the anecdote an edge: Will the kingfisher skewer the trout? Yet the effect of the sentence, capped off by two short sentences, is not of overwriting and a dramatic tease—the kingfisher leaves the trout unmolested—but of a lingering lyric. The final sentence defines in six short words the underlying theme of the story, the restoration of the spirit by fishing. Try reading it aloud and pause at each comma.

> As the shadow of the kingfisher moved up the stream, a big trout shot upstream in a long angle, only his shadow marking the angle, then lost his shadow as he came through the surface of the water, caught the sun, and then, as he went back into the stream under the surface, his shadow seemed to float down the stream with the current, unresisting, to his post under the bridge where he tightened, facing up into the current.

Nick's heart tightened as the trout moved. He felt all the old feeling.

An early draft had Nick feel "all the old thrill," a near cliché that would have restricted the meaning to fishing. The revised version raises the possibility that Nick has regained a lost ability to feel as he once did.

"The Toughest Town in Michigan"

Seney, my second stop, was once known as "Hell Town in the Pine," a raucous collection of loggers and women of loose virtue; the ladies, according to tales spun for naive visitors, were kept in a locked stockade guarded by mastiff dogs. In an early draft, one of Nick's fishing buddies remarks, "This was the toughest town in Michigan." The population once reached three thousand, double that during a log drive. Today's Seney, with fewer than two hundred residents, amounts to a scattering of homes, a couple of motels and cabin resorts, one bar, two gasoline stations, and two major landmarks. One is Highway 28, which runs straight through town, part of the infamous "Seney Stretch" that extends for twenty-five miles without a curve through monotonous swamplands. The other is the single railroad track that also runs straight through town, just south of and parallel to the highway. The rails are shiny from use, but an old railroad depot has been turned into a museum, seldom open, with a section of rusted track on exhibit.

A venerable steel bridge carries the track over the Fox River about halfway through town, a feature that many readers will remember from the opening scene of the story, when Nick stands on the bridge, looks down at trout in the river, and, after long absence from woods and waters, finds them "very satisfactory." It was natural to go there to look at the water below, as I did after arrival, just like Nick. The river remains, though trout no longer hold in such an accessible spot—and the river has fewer of them, as I would shortly find out. The water is a light root beer color. The bottom is sandy, not pebbly, as in the story. Beyond the town, the steep banks are so thick with trees, deadwood, and undergrowth that you need to wade the river to fish it, and then you encounter logjams, mud, and few places where you can make a cast without hanging up your fly. Local guides say not to bother fishing it, but I tried: I struggled down the bank, dealt with mud and fallen timber, and managed a cast over a small rising brook trout that had no interest in my dry fly. I quit, and struggled back up the bank. The Fox River, though, has numerous branches and tributaries, including the East and West branches and the Little Fox, which form a watery maze farther north. In a postcard addressed to his father, Dr. Clarence E. Hemingway, and postmarked from Seney on August 27, 1919, Hemingway said he and two friends were just back from a week's fishing "10 miles north in Schoolcraft Co.," presumably measuring from town, an area that includes all the branches. Hemingway added that he'd caught twenty-seven trout the day before, the "smallest nine inches." In a letter to a friend after the trip, Hemingway reported that he and his friends had fished more than one branch.

On my last day there, I visited the East Branch of the Fox and had a shock of recognition. The East Branch has all the settings from the story: meadows marked by ferns and slightly raised islands of pine, long stretches of open water, wide pools, and a cedar swamp. It fishes well, the local guides say, but I was out of time. Hemingway fictionalized his trip, writing his father that he had made up the entire story, but much of his writing is close to experience, and the landscape of the East Branch perfectly reflects the story. The case for the East Branch would become more solid at my final stop.

"A Kind of Desperate Dream River"

The Ernest and Mary Hemingway House, in Ketchum, sits high on a ridge overlooking a small island, a wild tangle of cottonwood, aspen, and brush created by a fork in the Big Wood River and inhabited, when I was there, by a herd of elk. The bulls bugled in the evening, and when I fished the river for rainbow trout, successfully, I kept coming upon small elk bands that noisily moved off into the brush. The house is 1950s Sun Valley architecture: the exterior is of cast concrete stained brown to look like timbers, accented by green molding and decking. Hemingway bought the place in 1959 and lived there with his wife Mary for the last two troubled years of his life: the house is full of their possessions. The writer's apartment was converted from a large garage at basement level and looks out through floor-to-ceiling glass doors, which can be fully and gratefully opened in fine weather, to the sloping ridge and wooded island below. It's a place to be quiet, write, and absorb what Hemingway experienced.

Sadly, an empty rod sock and a tattered fishnet are the only fishing gear in the house. After the Railroad Express Agency lost a Hemingway trunk full of his fishing gear on a trip west in 1940 or '41, he never fly-fished in Idaho again, according to a 1972 letter to *Field & Stream* magazine from his son Jack. "A Hardy Fairy, one of only two surviving items of trout fishing tackle, owned by my father the late Ernest Hemingway, is the one with which he fished on the lower Cottonwoods section of the Big Wood River on the one occasion that he trout fished here in Idaho . . . The balance of his tackle a trunk full of flies and other tackle items were lost the following year by Railway Express Company." The Hardy rod and letter are kept by the American Museum of Fly Fishing, in Manchester, Vermont.

The Community Library, in Ketchum, has a large collection of Hemingway materials left by numerous donors and by Mary, who lived there and in New York City until her death in 1986: most of what Mary left is in the Hemingway house. Before heading for Ketchum, I learned that the library staff had begun to sort more than forty boxes of materials recently donated by David Meeker, a lifelong Hemingway buff, collector, and dealer. I called ahead and asked if there were any references in those materials to "Big Two-Hearted River," and when the answer came back yes—there were letters and a map—I asked if they could be taken out for me to examine when I arrived, and again the answer was yes. When I got a look at the documents, they opened a new window on Seney and Hemingway's trip there.

A few years after Hemingway's death in 1961, his brother-in-law Sterling S. Sanford, widower of Hemingway's older sister, Marcelline, corresponded with a researcher who was trying to determine whether the Big Two-Hearted River, a daunting hike from Seney, was the river Hemingway had fished on his 1919 trip. The researcher, Donald M. St. John, had concluded that the river in the story was a "composite, a kind of desperate dream river which awaits every man when the rest of the world is going to hell." St. John also corresponded in the 1960s with John J. "Jack" Riordan, who had lived in Seney since 1916 and who wrote that there had been several forest fires around the town in 1918, later changing the date to 1919, and provided a hand-drawn map with more than half a dozen fire perimeters outlined near and into Seney, some labeled "old pine burning" and others "burned in 1919." (He also reported the burning of the wooden White House hotel around that same time.) Riordan said the East Branch had a dam about four and a half miles north from Seney, and Nick Adams fought his big trout in a deep, dammed-up pool: it's a match with the story, whether that was the actual spot or not. Riordan said he'd read little of Hemingway and couldn't say for certain where he had fished. But the evidence for the East Branch is considerable.

When I finished with the Riordan documents, it marked the end of a long trail that had begun with the rediscovery of a life-changing story from more than a half century earlier. I'd thought "Big Two-Hearted River" a perfect story back then, but the trail led to a deeper and better understanding of it. Reading Hemingway's own comments about it and the analysis of others was an essential start. But direct contact with its physical realities had greater impact, from viewing the handwritten drafts to standing in a meadow of green ferns punctuated by gray, century-old stumps to spending a week in the writer's apartment at the Hemingway House. All these elements and more came together one crisp fall day that Hemingway would have loved, when the trail led me to the island wilderness below the house. There, with a fly rod in hand and a fish on the line, I felt closer than ever before to the midwestern boy who took his troubles to the river and came away with his spirit restored and old feeling regained.

John N. Maclean
Ketchum, Idaho

Acknowledgments and Notes

The staffs of the John F. Kennedy Presidential Library and Museum, in Boston, and The Community Library, in Ketchum, provided invaluable assistance. Savannah York and Stacey Chandler at the JFK Library were helpful in making materials readily available. At The Community Library, Kelley Moulton, the Regional History Librarian, interrupted her work on the David Meeker papers to pull out documents from them for me; Pam Parker, a fisherwoman and library staffer, dug up the information about the loss of Hemingway's fishing gear; and Martha Williams, the programs and education director, worked daily to make my visit more productive and meaningful.

Bryan Whitledge, Public Service Librarian and Archivist for the Clarke Historical Library at Central Michigan University, Mt. Pleasant, Michigan, pointed me to the postcard Hemingway wrote his father from Seney in August 1919, which establishes the dates of the fishing trip and where Hemingway fished. The postcard is part of a collection the Clarke library purchased from a Hemingway family member in 2006.

Thanks also to Maggie Doherty, a writer who has lived in the Upper Peninsula, whose comments were insightful and helpful.

Big Two-Hearted River

PART
1

The train went on up the track out of sight, around one of the hills of burnt timber. Nick sat down on the bundle of canvas and bedding the baggage man had pitched out of the door of the baggage car. There was no town, nothing but the rails and the burned-over country. The thirteen saloons that had lined the one street of Seney had not left a trace. The foundations of the Mansion House hotel stuck up above the ground. The stone was chipped and split by the fire. It was all that was left of the town of Seney. Even the surface had been burned off the ground.

Nick looked at the burned-out stretch of hillside, where he had expected to find the scattered houses of the town and then walked down the railroad track to the bridge over the river. The river was there. It swirled against the log spiles of the bridge. Nick looked down into the clear, brown water, colored from the pebbly bottom, and watched the trout keeping themselves steady in the current with wavering fins. As he watched them they changed their positions by quick angles, only to hold steady in the fast water again. Nick watched them a long time.

He watched them holding themselves with their noses into the current, many trout in deep, fast moving water, slightly distorted as he watched far down through the glassy convex surface of the pool, its surface pushing and swelling smooth against the resistance of the log-driven spiles of the bridge. At the bottom of the pool were the big trout. Nick did

not see them at first. Then he saw them at the bottom of the pool, big trout looking to hold themselves on the gravel bottom in a varying mist of gravel and sand, raised in spurts by the current.

Nick looked down into the pool from the bridge. It was a hot day. A kingfisher flew up the stream. It was a long time since Nick had looked into a stream and seen trout. They were very satisfactory. As the shadow of the kingfisher moved up the stream, a big trout shot upstream in a long angle, only his shadow marking the angle, then lost his shadow as he came through the surface of the water, caught the sun, and then, as he went back into the stream under the surface, his shadow seemed to float down the stream with the current, unresisting, to his post under the bridge where he tightened, facing up into the current.

Nick's heart tightened as the trout moved. He felt all the old feeling.

He turned and looked down the stream. It stretched away, pebbly-bottomed with shallows and big boulders and a deep pool as it curved away around the foot of a bluff.

Nick walked back up the ties to where his pack lay in the cinders beside the railway track. He was

happy. He adjusted the pack harness around the bundle, pulling straps tight, slung the pack on his back, got his arms through the shoulder straps and took some of the pull off his shoulders by leaning his forehead against the wide band of the tump-line. Still, it was too heavy. It was much too heavy. He had his leather rod-case in his hand and leaning forward to keep the weight of the pack high on his shoulders he walked along the road that paralleled the railway track, leaving the burned town behind in the heat, and then turned off around a hill with a high, fire-scarred hill on either side onto a road that went back into the country. He walked along the road feeling the ache from the pull of the heavy pack. The road climbed steadily. It was hard work walking uphill. His muscles ached and the day was hot, but Nick felt happy. He felt he had left every-thing behind, the need for thinking, the need to write, other needs. It was all back of him.

From the time he had gotten down off the train and the baggage man had thrown his pack out of the open car door things had been different. Seney was burned, the country was burned over and changed, but it did not matter. It could not all be burned. He knew that. He hiked along the road, sweating in the sun, climbing to cross the range of hills that separated the railway from the pine plains.

The road ran on, dipping occasionally, but always climbing. Nick went on up. Finally the road, after going parallel to the burnt hillside, reached the top. Nick leaned back against a stump and slipped out of the pack harness. Ahead of him, as far as he could see, was the pine plain. The burned country stopped off at the left with the range of hills. On ahead islands of dark pine trees rose out of the plain. Far off to the left was the line of the river. Nick followed it with his eye and caught glints of the water in the sun.

There was nothing but the pine plain ahead of him, until the far blue hills that marked the Lake Superior height of land. He could hardly see them, faint and far away in the heat-light over the plain. If he looked too steadily they were gone. But if he only half-looked they were there, the far-off hills of the height of land.

Nick sat down against the charred stump and smoked a cigarette. His pack balanced on the top of the stump, harness holding ready, a hollow molded in it from his back. Nick sat smoking, looking out over the country. He did not need to get his map out. He knew where he was from the position of the river.

As he smoked, his legs stretched out in front of him, he noticed a grasshopper walk along the ground and up onto his woolen sock. The grasshopper was black. As he had walked along the road, climbing, he had started many grasshoppers from the dust. They were all black. They were not the big grasshoppers with yellow and black or red and black wings whirring out from their black wing sheathing as they fly up. These were just ordinary hoppers, but all a sooty black in color. Nick had wondered about them as he walked, without really thinking about them. Now, as he watched the black hopper that was nibbling at the wool of his sock with its four-way lip, he realized that they had all turned black from living in the burned-over land. He realized that the fire must have come the year before, but the grasshoppers were all black now. He wondered how long they would stay that way.

Carefully he reached his hand down and took hold of the hopper by the wings. He turned him up, all his legs walking in the air, and looked at his jointed belly. Yes, it was black too, iridescent where the back and head were dusty.

"Go on, hopper," Nick said, speaking out loud for the first time. "Fly away somewhere."

He tossed the grasshopper up into the air and watched him sail away to a charcoal stump across the road.

Nick stood up. He leaned his back against the weight of his pack where it rested upright on the stump and got his arms through the shoulder straps. He stood with the pack on his back on the brow of the hill looking out across the country, toward the distant river and then struck down the hillside away from the road. Underfoot the ground was good walking. Two hundred yards down the hillside the fire line stopped. Then it was sweet fern,

growing ankle high, to walk through, and clumps of jack pines; a long undulating country with frequent rises and descents, sandy underfoot and the country alive again.

Nick kept his direction by the sun. He knew where he wanted to strike the river and he kept on through the pine plain, mounting small rises to see other rises ahead of him and sometimes from the top of a rise a great solid island of pines off to his right or his left. He broke off some sprigs of the heathery sweet fern, and put them under his pack straps. The chafing crushed it and he smelled it as he walked.

He was tired and very hot, walking across the uneven, shadeless pine plain. At any time he knew he could strike the river by turning off to his left. It could not be more than a mile away. But he kept on toward the north to hit the river as far upstream as he could go in one day's walking.

For some time as he walked Nick had been in

sight of one of the big islands of pine standing out above the rolling high ground he was crossing. He dipped down and then as he came slowly up to the crest of the ridge he turned and made toward the pine trees.

There was no underbrush in the island of pine trees. The trunks of the trees went straight up or slanted toward each other. The trunks were straight and brown without branches. The branches were high above. Some interlocked to make a solid shadow on the brown forest floor. Around the grove of trees was a bare space. It was brown and soft underfoot as Nick walked on it. This was the overlapping of the pine needle floor, extending out beyond the width of the high branches. The trees had grown tall and the branches moved high, leaving in the sun this bare space they had once covered with shadow. Sharp at the edge of this extension of the forest floor commenced the sweet fern.

Nick slipped off his pack and lay down in the shade. He lay on his back and looked up into the pine trees. His neck and back and the small of his back rested as he stretched. The earth felt good against his back. He looked up at the sky, through the branches, and then shut his eyes. He opened them and looked up again. There was a wind high up in the branches. He shut his eyes again and went to sleep.

Nick woke stiff and cramped. The sun was nearly down. His pack was heavy and the straps painful as he lifted it on. He leaned over with the pack on and picked up the leather rod-case and started out from the pine trees across the sweet fern swale, toward the river. He knew it could not be more than a mile.

He came down a hillside covered with stumps into a meadow. At the edge of the meadow flowed the river. Nick was glad to get to the river. He walked upstream through the meadow. His trousers were soaked with the dew as he walked. After the hot day, the dew had come quickly and heavily. The river made no sound. It was too fast and smooth. At the edge of the meadow, before he mounted to a piece of high ground to make camp, Nick looked down the river at the trout rising. They were rising to insects come from the swamp on the other side of the stream when the sun went down. The trout jumped out of water to take them. While Nick

walked through the little stretch of meadow along-
side the stream, trout had jumped high out of water.
Now as he looked down the river, the insects must
be settling on the surface, for the trout were feed-
ing steadily all down the stream. As far down the
long stretch as he could see, the trout were rising,
making circles all down the surface of the water, as
though it were starting to rain.

The ground rose, wooded and sandy, to overlook
the meadow, the stretch of river and the swamp.
Nick dropped his pack and rod-case and looked for
a level piece of ground. He was very hungry and he
wanted to make his camp before he cooked. Between two jack pines, the ground was quite level.
He took the ax out of the pack and chopped out
two projecting roots. That leveled a piece of ground
large enough to sleep on. He smoothed out the
sandy soil with his hand and pulled all the sweet
fern bushes by their roots. His hands smelled good

from the sweet fern. He smoothed the uprooted earth. He did not want anything making lumps under the blankets. When he had the ground smooth, he spread his three blankets. One he folded double, next to the ground. The other two he spread on top.

With the ax he slit off a bright slab of pine from one of the stumps and split it into pegs for the tent. He wanted them long and solid to hold in the ground. With the tent unpacked and spread on the ground, the pack, leaning against a jackpine, looked much smaller. Nick tied the rope that served the tent for a ridgepole to the trunk of one of the pine trees and pulled the tent up off the ground with the other end of the rope and tied it to the other pine. The tent hung on the rope like a canvas blanket on a clothesline. Nick poked a pole he had cut up under the back peak of the canvas and then made it a tent by pegging out the sides. He pegged the sides out taut and drove the pegs

deep, hitting them down into the ground with the flat of the ax until the rope loops were buried and the canvas was drum tight.

Across the open mouth of the tent Nick fixed cheesecloth to keep out mosquitoes. He crawled inside under the mosquito bar with various things from the pack to put at the head of the bed under the slant of the canvas. Inside the tent the light came through the brown canvas. It smelled pleasantly of canvas. Already there was something mysterious and homelike. Nick was happy as he crawled inside the tent. He had not been unhappy all day. This was different though. Now things were done. There had been this to do. Now it was done. It had been a hard trip. He was very tired. That was done. He had made his camp. He was settled. Nothing could touch him. It was a good place to camp. He was there, in the good place. He was in his home where he had made it. Now he was hungry.

He came out, crawling under the cheesecloth. It was quite dark outside. It was lighter in the tent.

Nick went over to the pack and found, with his fingers, a long nail in a paper sack of nails, in the bottom of the pack. He drove it into the pine tree, holding it close and hitting it gently with the flat of the ax. He hung the pack up on the nail. All his supplies were in the pack. They were off the ground and sheltered now.

Nick was hungry. He did not believe he had ever been hungrier. He opened and emptied a can of pork and beans and a can of spaghetti into the frying pan.

"I've got a right to eat this kind of stuff, if I'm willing to carry it," Nick said. His voice sounded strange in the darkening woods. He did not speak again.

He started a fire with some chunks of pine he got with the ax from a stump. Over the fire he stuck a wire grill, pushing the four legs down into the ground with his boot. Nick put the frying pan on the grill over the flames. He was hungrier. The beans and spaghetti warmed. Nick stirred them and mixed them together. They began to bubble, making little bubbles that rose with difficulty to the surface. There was a good smell. Nick got out a bottle of tomato catchup and cut four slices of bread. The little bubbles were coming faster now. Nick sat down beside the fire and lifted the frying pan off. He poured about half the contents out into the tin plate. It spread slowly on the plate. Nick knew it was too hot. He poured on some tomato catchup. He knew the beans and spaghetti were still too hot. He looked at the fire, then at the tent, he was not going to spoil it all by burning his tongue. For years he had never enjoyed fried bananas because he had never been able to wait for them to cool. His tongue was very sensitive. He was very hungry. Across the river in the swamp, in the almost dark, he saw a mist rising. He looked at the tent once more. All right. He took a full spoonful from the plate.

"Chrise," Nick said, "Geezus Chrise," he said happily.

He ate the whole plateful before he remembered the bread. Nick finished the second plateful with the bread, mopping the plate shiny. He had not eaten since a cup of coffee and a ham sandwich in the station restaurant at St. Ignace. It had been a very fine experience. He had been that hungry before, but had not been able to satisfy it. He could have made camp hours before if he had wanted to. There were plenty of good places to camp on the river. But this was good.

Nick tucked two big chips of pine under the grill. The fire flared up. He had forgotten to get water for the coffee. Out of the pack he got a folding canvas bucket and walked down the hill, across the edge of the meadow, to the stream. The other bank was in the white mist. The grass was wet and cold as he knelt on the bank and dipped the canvas bucket into the stream. It bellied and pulled hard in the current. The water was ice cold. Nick rinsed the bucket and carried it full up to the camp. Up away from the stream it was not so cold.

Nick drove another big nail and hung up the bucket full of water. He dipped the coffeepot half full, put some more chips under the grill onto the fire and put the pot on. He could not remember which way he made coffee. He could remember an

argument about it with Hopkins, but not which side he had taken. He decided to bring it to a boil. He remembered now that was Hopkins's way. He had once argued about everything with Hopkins. While he waited for the coffee to boil, he opened a small can of apricots. He liked to open cans. He emptied the can of apricots out into a tin cup. While he watched the coffee on the fire, he drank the juice syrup of the apricots, carefully at first to keep from spilling, then meditatively, sucking the apricots down. They were better than fresh apricots.

The coffee boiled as he watched. The lid came up and coffee and grounds ran down the side of the pot. Nick took it off the grill. It was a triumph for Hopkins. He put sugar in the empty apricot cup and poured some of the coffee out to cool. It was too hot to pour and he used his hat to hold the handle of the coffeepot. He would not let it steep in the pot at all. Not the first cup. It should be straight

Hopkins all the way. Hop deserved that. He was a very serious coffee maker. He was the most serious man Nick had ever known. Not heavy, serious. That was a long time ago. Hopkins spoke without moving his lips. He had played polo. He made millions of dollars in Texas. He had borrowed carfare to go to Chicago, when the wire came that his first big well had come in. He could have wired for money. That would have been too slow. They called Hop's girl the Blonde Venus. Hop did not mind because she was not his real girl. Hopkins said very confidently that none of them would make fun of his real girl. He was right. Hopkins went away when the telegram came. That was on the Black River. It took eight days for the telegram to reach him. Hopkins gave away his .22 caliber Colt automatic pistol to Nick. He gave his camera to Bill. It was to remember him always by. They were all going fishing again next summer. The Hop Head was rich. He would get a yacht and they would all cruise along the north shore of Lake Superior. He was excited but serious. They said good-by and all felt bad. It broke up the trip. They never saw Hopkins again. That was a long time ago on the Black River.

Nick drank the coffee, the coffee according to Hopkins. The coffee was bitter. Nick laughed. It made a good ending to the story. His mind was starting to work. He knew he could choke it because he was tired enough. He spilled the coffee out of the pot and shook the grounds loose into the fire. He lit a cigarette and went inside the tent. He took off his shoes and trousers, sitting on the blankets, rolled the shoes up inside the trousers for a pillow and got in between the blankets.

Out through the front of the tent he watched the glow of the fire, when the night wind blew on it. It was a quiet night. The swamp was perfectly quiet. Nick stretched under the blanket comfortably.

A mosquito hummed close to his ear. Nick sat up and lit a match. The mosquito was on the canvas, over his head. Nick moved the match quickly up to it. The mosquito made a satisfactory hiss in the flame. The match went out. Nick lay down again under the blankets. He turned on his side and shut his eyes. He was sleepy. He felt sleep coming. He curled up under the blanket and went to sleep.

PART
2

In the morning the sun was up and the tent was starting to get hot. Nick crawled out under the mosquito netting stretched across the mouth of the tent to look at the morning. The grass was wet on his hands as he came out. He held his trousers and his shoes in his hands. The sun was just up over the hill. There was the meadow, the river and the swamp. There were birch trees in the green of the swamp on the other side of the river.

The river was clear and smoothly fast in the early morning. Down about two hundred yards were three logs all the way across the stream. They made the water smooth and deep above them. As Nick watched, a mink crossed the river on the logs and went into the swamp. Nick was excited. He was excited by the early morning and the river. He was really too hurried to eat breakfast, but he knew he must. He built a little fire and put on the coffeepot. While the water was heating in the pot he took an empty bottle and went down over the edge of the high ground to the meadow. The meadow was wet with dew and Nick wanted to catch grasshoppers for bait before the sun dried the grass. He found plenty of good grasshoppers. They were at the base of the grass stems. Sometimes they clung to a grass stem. They were cold and wet with the dew and could not jump until the sun warmed them. Nick picked them up, taking only the medium-sized brown ones, and put them into the bottle. He turned over a log and just under the shelter of the edge were several hundred hoppers. It was a grasshopper lodging house. Nick put about fifty of the medium browns into the bottle. While he was picking up the hoppers the others warmed in the sun and commenced to hop away. They flew when they hopped. At first they made one flight and stayed stiff when they landed, as though they were dead.

Nick knew that by the time he was through with breakfast they would be as lively as ever. Without dew in the grass it would take him all day to catch a bottle full of good grasshoppers and he would have to crush many of them, slamming at them with his hat. He washed his hands at the stream. He was excited to be near it. Then he walked up to the tent. The hoppers were already jumping stiffly in the grass. In the bottle, warmed by the sun, they were jumping in a mass. Nick put in a pine stick as a cork. It plugged the mouth of the bottle enough so the hoppers could not get out, and left plenty of air passage.

He had rolled the log back and knew he could get grasshoppers there every morning.

Nick laid the bottle full of jumping grasshoppers against a pine trunk. Rapidly he mixed some buckwheat flour with water and stirred it smooth, one cup of flour, one cup of water. He put a handful of coffee in the pot and dipped a lump of grease out of a can and slid it sputtering across the hot skillet. On the smoking skillet he poured smoothly the buckwheat batter. It spread like lava, the grease spitting sharply. Around the edges the buckwheat cake began to firm, then brown, then crisp. The surface was bubbling slowly to porousness. Nick pushed under the browned undersurface with a fresh pine chip. He shook the skillet sideways and the cake was loose on the surface. I won't try and flop it, he thought. He slid the chip of clean wood all the way under the cake, and flopped it over onto its face. It sputtered in the pan.

When it was cooked Nick regreased the skillet. He used all the batter. It made another big flapjack and one smaller one.

Nick ate a big flapjack and a smaller one, covered with apple butter. He put apple butter on the third cake, folded it over twice, wrapped it in oiled paper and put it in his shirt pocket. He put the apple butter jar back in the pack and cut bread for two sandwiches.

In the pack he found a big onion. He sliced it in two and peeled the silky outer skin. Then he cut one half into slices and made onion sandwiches. He wrapped them in oiled paper and buttoned them in the other pocket of his khaki shirt. He turned the skillet upside down on the grill, drank the coffee, sweetened and yellow brown with the condensed milk in it, and tidied up the camp. It was a nice little camp.

Nick took his fly rod out of the leather rod-case, jointed it, and shoved the rod-case back into the tent. He put on the reel and threaded the line through the guides. He had to hold it from hand to hand, as he threaded it, or it would slip back through its own weight. It was a heavy, double-tapered fly line. Nick had paid eight dollars for it a long time ago. It was made heavy to lift back in the air and come forward flat and heavy and straight to make it possible to cast a fly which has no weight. Nick opened the aluminum leader box. The leaders were coiled between the damp flannel pads. Nick had wet the pads at the water cooler on the train up to St. Ignace. In the damp pads the gut leaders had softened and Nick unrolled one and tied it by a loop at the end to the heavy fly line. He fastened a hook on the end of the leader. It was a small hook, very thin and springy.

Nick took it from his hook book, sitting with the rod across his lap. He tested the knot and the spring of the rod by pulling the line taut. It was a good feeling. He was careful not to let the hook bite into his finger.

He started down to the stream, holding his rod, the bottle of grasshoppers hung from his neck by a thong tied in half hitches around the neck of the bottle. His landing net hung by a hook from his belt. Over his shoulder was a long flour sack tied at each corner into an ear. The cord went over his shoulder. The sack flapped against his legs.

Nick felt awkward and professionally happy with all his equipment hanging from him. The grasshopper bottle swung against his chest. In his shirt the breast pockets bulged against him with the lunch and his fly book.

He stepped into the stream. It was a shock. His trousers clung tight to his legs. His shoes felt the gravel. The water was a rising cold shock.

Rushing, the current sucked against his legs.

Where he stepped in, the water was over his knees. He waded with the current. The gravel slid under his shoes. He looked down at the swirl of water below each leg and tipped up the bottle to get a grasshopper.

The first grasshopper gave a jump in the neck of the bottle and went out into the water. He was sucked under in the whirl by Nick's right leg and came to the surface a little way down stream. He floated rapidly, kicking. In a quick circle, breaking the smooth surface of the water, he disappeared. A trout had taken him.

Another hopper poked his face out of the bottle. His antennae wavered. He was getting his front legs out of the bottle to jump. Nick took him by the head and held him while he threaded the slim hook under his chin, down through his thorax and into the last segments of his abdomen. The grasshopper took hold of the hook with his front feet,

spitting tobacco juice on it. Nick dropped him into the water.

Holding the rod in his right hand he let out line against the pull of the grasshopper in the current. He stripped off line from the reel with his left hand and let it run free. He could see the hopper in the little waves of the current. It went out of sight.

There was a tug on the line. Nick pulled against the taut line. It was his first strike. Holding the now living rod across the current, he brought in the line with his left hand. The rod bent in jerks, the trout pumping against the current. Nick knew it was a small one. He lifted the rod straight up in the air. It bowed with the pull.

He saw the trout in the water jerking with his head and body against the shifting tangent of the line in the stream.

Nick took the line in his left hand and pulled the trout, thumping tiredly against the current, to the surface. His back was mottled the clear, water-over-gravel color, his side flashing in the sun. The rod under his right arm, Nick stooped, dipping his right hand into the current. He held the trout, never still, with his moist right hand, while he unhooked the barb from his mouth, then dropped him back into the stream.

He hung unsteadily in the current, then settled to the bottom beside a stone. Nick reached down his hand to touch him, his arm to the elbow under-water. The trout was steady in the moving stream, resting on the gravel, beside a stone. As Nick's fingers touched him, touched his smooth, cool, underwater feeling, he was gone, gone in a shadow across the bottom of the stream.

He's all right, Nick thought. He was only tired.

He had wet his hand before he touched the trout, so he would not disturb the delicate mucus that covered him. If a trout was touched with a dry hand, a white fungus attacked the unprotected spot. Years before when he had fished crowded streams, with fly fishermen ahead of him and behind him, Nick had again and again come on dead trout, furry with white fungus, drifted against a rock, or floating belly up in some pool. Nick did not like to fish with other men on the river. Unless they were of your party, they spoiled it.

He wallowed down the stream, above his knees in the current, through the fifty yards of shallow water above the pile of logs that crossed the stream. He did not rebait his hook and held it in his hand as he waded. He was certain he could catch small trout in the shallows, but he did not want them. There would be no big trout in the shallows this time of day.

Now the water deepened up his thighs sharply and coldly. Ahead was the smooth dammed-back flood of water above the logs. The water was smooth and dark; on the left, the lower edge of the meadow; on the right, the swamp.

Nick leaned back against the current and took a hopper from the bottle. He threaded the hopper on the hook and spat on him for good luck. Then he pulled several yards of line from the reel and tossed the hopper out ahead onto the fast, dark water. It floated down toward the logs, then the weight of the line pulled the bait under the surface. Nick held the rod in his right hand, letting the line run out through his fingers.

There was a long tug. Nick struck and the rod came alive and dangerous, bent double, the line tightening, coming out of water, tightening, all in a heavy, dangerous, steady pull. Nick felt the moment when the leader would break if the strain increased and let the line go.

The reel ratcheted into a mechanical shriek as the line went out in a rush. Too fast. Nick could not check it, the line rushing out, the reel note rising as the line ran out.

With the core of the reel showing, his heart feeling stopped with the excitement, leaning back against the current that mounted icily his thighs, Nick thumbed the reel hard with his left hand. It was awkward getting his thumb inside the fly reel frame.

As he put on pressure the line tightened into sudden hardness and beyond the logs a huge trout went high out of the water. As he jumped, Nick lowered the tip of the rod. But he felt, as he dropped the tip to ease the strain, the moment when the strain was too great, the hardness too tight. Of course, the leader had broken. There was no mistaking the feeling when all spring left the line and it became dry and hard. Then it went slack.

His mouth dry, his heart down, Nick reeled in. He had never seen so big a trout. There was a

heaviness, a power not to be held, and then the bulk of him, as he jumped. He looked as broad as a salmon.

Nick's hand was shaky. He reeled in slowly. The thrill had been too much. He felt, vaguely, a little sick, as though it would be better to sit down.

The leader had broken where the hook was tied to it. Nick took it in his hand. He thought of the trout somewhere on the bottom, holding himself steady over the gravel, far down below the light, under the logs, with the hook in his jaw. Nick knew the trout's teeth would cut through the snell of the hook. The hook would imbed itself in his jaw. He'd bet the trout was angry. Anything that size would be angry. That was a trout. He had been solidly hooked. Solid as a rock. He felt like a rock, too, before he started off. By God, he was a big one. By God, he was the biggest one I ever heard of.

Nick climbed out onto the meadow and stood,

water running down his trousers and out of his shoes, his shoes squelchy. He went over and sat on the logs. He did not want to rush his sensations any.

He wriggled his toes in the water, in his shoes, and got out a cigarette from his breast pocket. He lit it and tossed the match into the fast water below the logs. A tiny trout rose at the match, as it swung around in the fast current. Nick laughed. He would finish the cigarette.

He sat on the logs, smoking, drying in the sun, the sun warm on his back, the river shallow ahead, entering the woods, curving into the woods, shallows, light glittering, big water-smooth rocks, cedars along the bank and white birches, the logs warm in the sun, smooth to sit on, without bark, gray to the touch; slowly the feeling of disappointment left him. It went away slowly, the feeling of disappointment that came sharply after the thrill that made his shoulders ache. It was all right now. His rod lying out on the logs, Nick tied a new hook on the leader, pulling the gut tight until it grimped into itself in a hard knot.

He baited up, then picked up the rod and walked to the far end of the logs to get into the water, where it was not too deep. Under and beyond the logs was a deep pool. Nick walked around the shallow shelf near the swamp shore until he came out on the shallow bed of the stream.

On the left, where the meadow ended and the woods began, a great elm tree was uprooted. Gone over in a storm, it lay back into the woods, its roots clotted with dirt, grass growing in them, rising a solid bank beside the stream. The river cut to the edge of the uprooted tree. From where Nick stood he could see deep channels, like ruts, cut in the shallow bed of the stream by the flow of the current. Pebbly where he stood and pebbly and full of boulders beyond; where it curved near the tree roots, the bed of the stream was marly and between the ruts of deep water green weed fronds swung in the current.

Nick swung the rod back over his shoulder and forward, and the line, curving forward, laid the grasshopper down on one of the deep channels in the weeds. A trout struck and Nick hooked him.

Holding the rod far out toward the uprooted tree and sloshing backward in the current, Nick worked the trout, plunging, the rod bending alive, out of the danger of the weeds into the open river. Holding the rod, pumping alive against the current, Nick brought the trout in. He rushed, but always came, the spring of the rod yielding to the rushes, sometimes jerking underwater, but always bringing him in. Nick eased downstream with the rushes. The rod above his head, he led the trout over the net, then lifted.

The trout hung heavy in the net, mottled trout back and silver sides in the meshes. Nick unhooked him; heavy sides, good to hold, big undershot jaw; and slipped him, heaving and big, sliding, into the long sack that hung from his shoulders in the water.

Nick spread the mouth of the sack against the current and it filled, heavy with water. He held it up, the bottom in the stream, and the water poured out through the sides. Inside at the bottom was the big trout, alive in the water.

Nick moved downstream. The sack out ahead of him, sunk, heavy in the water, pulling from his shoulders.

It was getting hot, the sun hot on the back of his neck.

Nick had one good trout. He did not care about getting many trout. Now the stream was shallow and wide. There were trees along both banks. The trees of the left bank made short shadows on the current in the forenoon sun. Nick knew there were trout in each shadow. In the afternoon, after the sun had crossed toward the hills, the trout would be in the cool shadows on the other side of the stream.

The very biggest ones would lie up close to the bank. You could always pick them up there on the Black. When the sun was down they all moved out into the current. Just when the sun made the water blinding in the glare before it went down, you were liable to strike a big trout anywhere in the current. It was almost impossible to fish then, the surface of the water was blinding as a mirror in the sun. Of course, you could fish upstream, but in a stream like the Black, or this, you had to wallow against the current and in a deep place, the water piled up on you. It was no fun to fish upstream with this much current.

Nick moved along through the shallow stretch, watching the banks for deep holes. A beech tree grew close beside the river, so that the branches hung down into the water. The stream went back in under the leaves. There were always trout in a place like that.

Nick did not care about fishing that hole. He was sure he would get hooked in the branches.

It looked deep though. He dropped the grasshopper so the current took it underwater, back in under the overhanging branch. The line pulled hard and Nick struck. The trout threshed heavily, half out of water in the leaves and branches. The line was caught. Nick pulled hard and the trout was off. He reeled in and, holding the hook in his hand, walked down the stream.

Ahead, close to the left bank, was a big log. Nick saw it was hollow; pointing up river the current entered it smoothly, only a little ripple spread each side of the log. The water was deepening. The top of the hollow log was gray and dry. It was partly in the shadow.

Nick took the cork out of the grasshopper bottle

and a hopper clung to it. He picked him off, hooked him and tossed him out. He held the rod far out so that the hopper on the water moved into the current flowing into the hollow log. Nick lowered the rod and the hopper floated in. There was a heavy strike. Nick swung the rod against the pull. It felt as though he were hooked into the log itself, except for the live feeling.

He tried to force the fish out into the current. It came, heavily.

The line went slack and Nick thought the trout was gone. Then he saw him, very near, in the current, shaking his head, trying to get the hook out. His mouth was clamped shut. He was fighting the hook in the clear flowing current.

Looping in the line with his left hand, Nick swung the rod to make the line taut and tried to lead the trout toward the net, but he was gone, out of sight, the line pumping. Nick fought him against the current, letting him thump in the water against the spring of the rod. He shifted the rod to his left hand, worked the trout upstream, holding his weight, fighting on the rod, and then let him down into the net. He lifted him clear of the water, a heavy half circle in the net, the net dripping, unhooked him and slid him into the sack.

He spread the mouth of the sack and looked down in at the two big trout alive in the water.

Through the deepening water, Nick waded over to the hollow log. He took the sack off, over his head, the trout flopping as it came out of water, and hung it so the trout were deep in the water. Then he pulled himself up on the log and sat, the water from his trousers and boots running down into the stream. He laid his rod down, moved along to the shady end of the log and took the sandwiches out of his pocket. He dipped the sandwiches in the cold water. The current carried away the crumbs. He ate the sandwiches and dipped his hat full of water to drink, the water running out through his hat just ahead of his drinking.

It was cool in the shade, sitting on the log. He took a cigarette out and struck a match to light it. The match sunk into the gray wood, making a tiny furrow. Nick leaned over the side of the log, found a hard place and lit the match. He sat smoking and watching the river.

Ahead the river narrowed and went into a swamp. The river became smooth and deep and the swamp looked solid with cedar trees, their trunks close together, their branches solid. It would not be possible to walk through a swamp like that. The branches grew so low. You would have to keep almost level with the ground to move at all. You could not crash through the branches. That must be why the animals that lived in swamps were built the way they were, Nick thought.

He wished he had brought something to read. He felt like reading. He did not feel like going on into the swamp. He looked down the river. A big cedar slanted all the way across the stream. Beyond that the river went into the swamp.

Nick did not want to go in there now. He felt a reaction against deep wading with the water deepening up under his armpits, to hook big trout in places impossible to land them. In the swamp the banks were bare, the big cedars came together overhead, the sun did not come through, except in patches; in the fast deep water, in the half light, the fishing would be tragic. In the swamp fishing was a tragic adventure. Nick did not want it. He did not want to go down the stream any farther today.

He took out his knife, opened it and stuck it in the log. Then he pulled up the sack, reached into it and brought out one of the trout. Holding him near the tail, hard to hold, alive, in his hand, he whacked him against the log. The trout quivered, rigid. Nick laid him on the log in the shade and broke the neck of the other fish the same way. He laid them side by side on the log. They were fine trout.

Nick cleaned them, slitting them from the vent to the tip of the jaw. All the insides and the gills and tongue came out in one piece. They were both males; long gray-white strips of milt, smooth and clean. All the insides clean and compact, coming out all together. Nick tossed the offal ashore for the minks to find.

He washed the trout in the stream. When he held them back up in the water they looked like live fish. Their color was not gone yet. He washed his hands and dried them on the log. Then he laid the trout on the sack spread out on the log, rolled them up in it, tied the bundle and put it in the landing net. His knife was still standing, blade stuck in the log. He cleaned it on the wood and put it in his pocket.

Nick stood up on the log, holding his rod, the landing net hanging heavy, then stepped into the water and splashed ashore. He climbed the bank and cut up into the woods, toward the high ground. He was going back to camp. He looked back. The river just showed through the trees. There were plenty of days coming when he could fish the swamp.

Ernest Hemingway was awarded the Nobel Prize for Literature in 1954. His novels include *The Sun Also Rises, A Farewell to Arms, For Whom the Bell Tolls,* and *The Old Man and the Sea,* which won the Pulitzer Prize in 1953. Born in Oak Park, Illinois, in 1899, he died in Ketchum, Idaho, on July 2, 1961.

John N. Maclean is the author of the national bestseller *Home Waters,* a memoir of his family's four-generation connection to Montana's Blackfoot River, which his father, Norman Maclean, made famous in *A River Runs through It.* The younger Maclean spent thirty years at the *Chicago Tribune,* most of that time as a Washington correspondent. After leaving the *Tribune,* Maclean wrote five nonfiction books about wildland fire that are considered a staple of fire literature. An avid fly fisherman, he lives in Washington, DC, and at a family cabin in Montana.

Chris Wormell is a distinguished printmaker and illustrator. His book projects include *Teeth, Tails, and Tentacles,* which was named one of the Ten Best Illustrated Books of the Year by *The New York Times Book Review;* the illustrated editions of Philip Pullman's *His Dark Materials;* and two novels for children, *The Magic Place* and *The Lucky Bottle.* Wormell has been commissioned by the Royal Mail, the Aston Villa Football Club, the Folio Society, and the Royal Opera House.

About Mariner Books

Mariner Books traces its beginnings to 1832 when William Ticknor cofounded the Old Corner Bookstore in Boston, from which he would run the legendary firm Ticknor and Fields, publisher of Ralph Waldo Emerson, Harriet Beecher Stowe, Nathaniel Hawthorne, and Henry David Thoreau. Following Ticknor's death, Henry Oscar Houghton acquired Ticknor and Fields and, in 1880, formed Houghton Mifflin, which later merged with venerable Harcourt Publishing to form Houghton Mifflin Harcourt. HarperCollins purchased HMH's trade publishing business in 2021 and reestablished their storied lists and editorial team under the name Mariner Books.

Uniting the legacies of Houghton Mifflin, Harcourt Brace, and Ticknor and Fields, Mariner Books continues one of the great traditions in American bookselling. Our imprints have introduced an incomparable roster of enduring classics, including Hawthorne's *The Scarlet Letter,* Thoreau's *Walden,* Willa Cather's *O Pioneers!,* Virginia Woolf's *To the Lighthouse,* W.E.B. Du Bois's *Black Reconstruction,* J.R.R. Tolkien's *The Lord of the Rings,* Carson McCullers's *The Heart Is a Lonely Hunter,* Ann Petry's *The Narrows,* George Orwell's *Animal Farm* and *Nineteen Eighty-Four,* Rachel Carson's *Silent Spring,* Margaret Walker's *Jubilee,* Italo Calvino's *Invisible Cities,* Alice Walker's *The Color Purple,* Margaret Atwood's *The Handmaid's Tale,* Tim O'Brien's *The Things They Carried,* Philip Roth's *The Plot Against America,* Jhumpa Lahiri's *Interpreter of Maladies,* and many others. Today Mariner Books remains proudly committed to the craft of fine publishing established nearly two centuries ago at the Old Corner Bookstore.